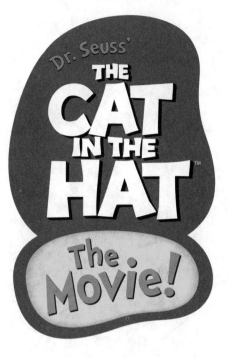

Adapted by Jesse Leon McCann
Based on the motion picture screenplay by
Alec Berg & David Mandel & Jeff Schaffer

Illustrated by Christopher Moroney

Based on the book by Dr. Seuss

www.universalstudios.com

www.randomhouse.com/seussville

This special edition was printed for Kohl's by Golden Books, an imprint of
Random House Children's Books, a division of Random House, Inc., New York.

The Walden household was in an uproar!
Mom was getting ready for her BIG party.
Deliverymen bustled in and out. And Conrad and
Sally were bickering—*again*.

Mom went to run some errands and left Mrs.
Kwan to baby-sit. "You two behave," Mom said.

No sooner had Mom left than Mrs. Kwan fell
into a deep sleep and began to snore.

It began to rain.

Conrad and Sally shifted and fidgeted.

"Quit bugging the fish," Sally snapped at Conrad.

"*You* quit it," Conrad snapped back.

Suddenly, they heard a loud *bump*—or was it a
thump?

"What was that?" whispered Sally.

Nevins, the dog, growled. Mrs. Kwan snored on.

Conrad and Sally crept slowly up the stairs to
investigate. They saw something big. Something
furry. It was . . .

A cat—*in a hat!*

"Aaaaagh!" they screamed.

"That could have gone better," remarked the Cat.

Conrad and Sally ran this-a-way and that-a-way.

But whichever way they turned, there he was.

"Who are you?" whimpered Sally.

"I'm the Cat in the Hat," said he with a bow.
"Nice place. You two must love it here."

"We're bored out of our minds!" said Conrad.

"But this house is full of fun," said the Cat. He
checked the kids with his phunometer. "Yep!" he
said. "You two have a classic case of the Worst-Day-
Evers. I know just the cure!"

"You kids need to forget about the rules and learn to have a little fun. The problem with you is that you're old before your time. You're way too uptight. You need to relax, kick back, chill out, pull out the stops . . .

". . . and enjoy yourself!"

"ALL RIGHT!" cried Conrad and Sally, getting into the spirit.

"Don't listen to him!" said the fish. "I have the feeling this cat is about to violate all seventeen of your mother's rules!"

Everyone turned to stare.

Why, that fish had never said a word before!

"I know!" said the Cat. "Let's make cupcakes!"
They mixed a pound of sugar, two sticks of butter, a
pile of hot dogs, ten peanuts, a rasher of bacon, and
a gaggle of grapes!

Then they poured the batter into cupcake tins
and slid the whole mess into the oven. What a
grand time they were having, until . . .

KA-BOOM! The oven exploded purple goop.
"Don't worry," said the Cat. "I'll clean this up."
He started swabbing up the gooey goop.
"That's not a towel!" cried Sally. "That's Mom's party dress!"
"We're doomed!" moaned the fish. "Oh, what will become of us?"

"Calm down!" said the Cat. "I have the answer
to all your cleaning needs."

The Cat went to the living room, where the kids
were forbidden to play, and opened a crate. Out
popped a pair of strange creatures.

Said the Cat, "Allow me to introduce you to . . .
Thing One and Thing Two. They'll have this place
cleaned up in no time."

The Things each grabbed one end of Mom's dress and snapped it. The stains flew off the dress—and landed on the couch!

"Are you sure these Things know what they're doing?" asked Sally nervously.

The Cat shrugged. "Sure, they're professionals."

Sally and Conrad tried to catch the Things, but they were very quick—and very tricky.

The Things ran up the walls and across the ceiling! They rode bikes over the furniture! They left purple tracks everywhere! That poor puppy dog Nevins headed for the hills.

"Why don't we pop outside, have a little fun, and grab the dog while we're at it?" asked the Cat. "Besides, it's too nice to stay inside."

"What are you talking about?" asked Sally. "It's pouring!"

But when the Cat opened the door, sunlight streamed in.

The search for Nevins led them to a neighbor's birthday party. The Cat thought it best for everyone to stay hidden. But he was quickly spotted by the kids!

Thinking fast, Conrad and Sally tossed candy
from behind the bushes. The kids dived into the
candy and forgot about the Cat—but during all the
commotion, Nevins ran off *again*!

That was when the Cat magically produced a
car. "It's my Super Luxurious Omnidirectional
Whatchamajigger, or S.L.O.W. for short. Grab a
steering wheel—we can all drive!"

Having three drivers in one car didn't work so well. *CRASH!!!*

"Wow! That was sweet!" cried Conrad happily.

Walking home, they spotted Nevins in a beauty shop and caught him. Now all they had to do was hurry home and clean before Mom came back.

But what a mess they found! Whatever were they to do now? When Mom came home, she would have a fit!

"How about a game of tennis?" asked the Cat.

That was the last straw.

"Get out!" shouted Conrad and Sally.

After the Cat left, Conrad said, "Why don't you go upstairs, Sally? I'll tell Mom it was all my fault."

"We should share the blame," Sally said. For the first time in a long time, she smiled at him and said, "By the way, you're a pretty good brother."

"I'm glad you think so," said Conrad, returning the smile.

Just then, the front door opened, and through it came . . .

. . . the Cat in the Hat—singing, and driving
his Super-Splendiferous Housecleaning Machine!
Conrad and Sally could scarcely believe their eyes.

When the cleaning crew had finished, the house was spotless. They'd dry-cleaned Mom's dress, scrubbed Conrad and Sally, and even given Nevins a bath—all without waking up Mrs. Kwan!

"Good-bye, Cat!" called Conrad and Sally.
"Thanks for everything!"
The Cat was still singing as he drove away.